For Rich and Juno,
who are just the way I love them.
x x x

Ingredients

🐝

little bee books

An imprint of Bonnier Publishing Group
853 Broadway, New York, NY 10003
Copyright © 2015 by Ciara Flood
First published in Great Britain by Templar Publishing
This little bee books edition, 2015.

www.littlebeebooks.com
www.bonnierpublishing.com

Ingredients

All rights reserved, including the right of
reproduction in whole or in part in any form.
LITTLE BEE BOOKS is a trademark of
Bonnier Publishing Group, and associated colophon
is a trademark of Bonnier Publishing Group.
Manufactured in China 0315008

First Edition 2 4 6 8 10 9 7 5 3 1
Library of Congress Control Number: 2014958646
ISBN 978-1-4998-0071-5

Ciara Flood

Those PESKY RABBITS

little bee books

Bear lived on his own
in the middle of nowhere,

and that was just
the way he liked it.

So, you can imagine how annoyed he was

when a family of rabbits
    built their house . . .

right next to his!

Soon after the rabbits had moved in there was a

KNOCK, KNOCK!

on his door.

"Hello, Mr. Bear.
Could we borrow
some honey please?
We want to bake
a cake!"

"I don't have **any honey**,"
Bear said.

"Pesky rabbits!" he muttered.
Bear poured himself a cup of tea,
then added a drop of milk and

**ten spoons
of honey.**

Delicious
Milk, Tea a
Hot Choco

with cheese
ers, and
grapes

Tasty w

Good with figs
and Raisins

YUMMY ON
PANCAKES

He was just about to sit down when . . .

KNOCK, KNOCK!

"Hello, Mr. Bear! Could you
help us chop some wood, please?"

"No," Bear said. "I'm far
too busy to help."

KNOCK, KNOCK!

After his tea, Bear had fallen asleep in front of his fire, when . . .

"What now?!"

he growled.

"Hello, Mr. Bear.
Would you like to swap
books with us?"

A little later, Bear had just started
to eat his dinner when . . .

KNOCK,
KNOCK!

"Hello, Mr. Bear.
Do you . . . wa-want to watch
sho-shooting stars with us?"

"No! No! No!"
Bear roared.

"What I **want** is to be **left alone!**"

So Bear got what he wanted.

Then one day, he heard a soft

KNOCK,
KNOCK!

But there were no
rabbits at his door,

just a basket.

Inside was a cake,
some wood, a book,
and a note.

The note read:

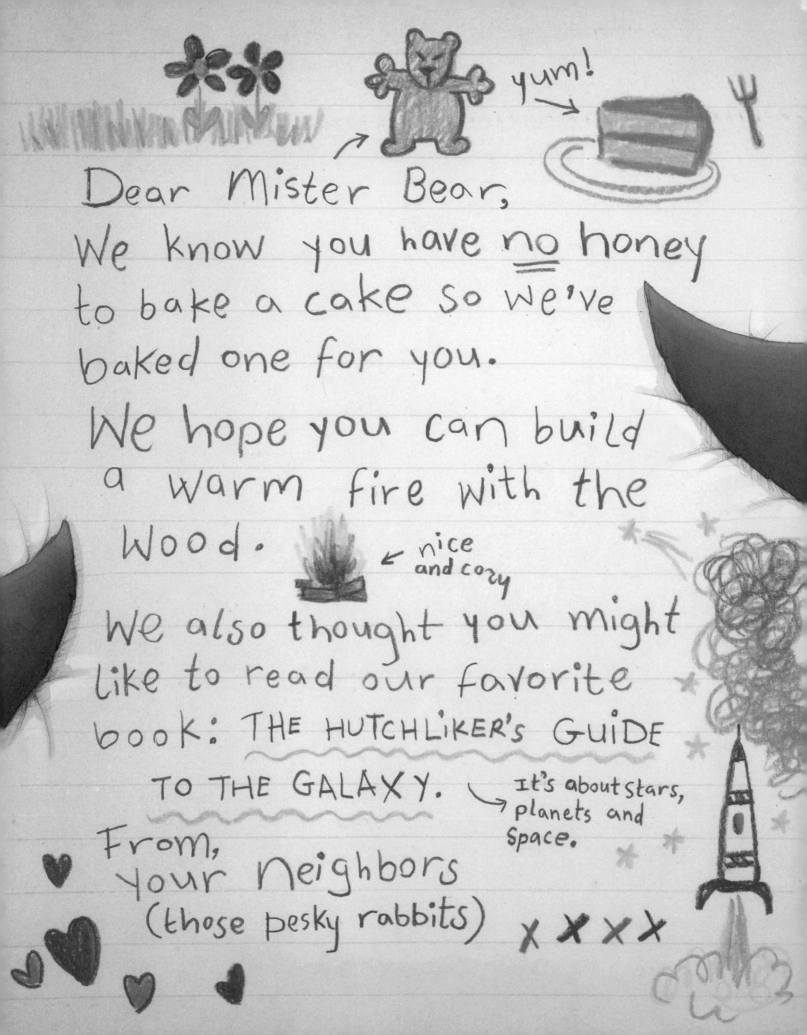

Dear Mister Bear,
We know you have <u>no</u> honey to bake a cake so we've baked one for you.

We hope you can build a warm fire with the wood.

← nice and cozy

We also thought you might like to read our favorite book: THE HUTCHLIKER's GUIDE TO THE GALAXY.

It's about stars, planets and space.

From,
Your Neighbors
(those pesky rabbits)

yum!

X X X X

Bear ate the cake,

made a fire with the wood,

and read the book
before bed.

But he couldn't fall asleep that night.
For the first time ever, Bear felt . . .

. . . lonely.

So he decided to do something he had never done before.

He went to visit his neighbors.

Bear spent a lot of time
with the rabbits after that.

And do you
know something?

That was just the way he liked it.